JER Portic
Portice, Michelle,
Kit and Kaboodle visit the farm /
$4.99
on1285691024
DISCARD
W9-DCL-609
3 4028 10767 2280
HARRIS COUNTY PUBLIC LIBRARY

VISIT THE FARM

By Michelle Portice
Art by Mitch Mortimer

HIGHLIGHTS PRESS
Honesdale, Pennsylvania

Stories + Puzzles = Reading Success!

Dear Parents,

Highlights Puzzle Readers are an innovative approach to learning to read that combines puzzles and stories to build motivated, confident readers.

Developed in collaboration with reading experts, the stories and puzzles are seamlessly integrated so that readers are encouraged to read the story, solve the puzzles, and then read the story again. This helps increase vocabulary and reading fluency and creates a satisfying reading experience for any kind of learner. In addition, solving Hidden Pictures puzzles fosters important reading and learning skills such as:

- shape and letter recognition
- sound-letter relationships
- visual discrimination
- logic
- flexible thinking
- sequencing

With high-interest stories, humorous characters, and trademark puzzles, Highlights Puzzle Readers offer a winning combination for inspiring young learners to love reading.

This is Kit.
This is Kaboodle.
They love to travel. You can help them on each adventure.
As you read the story, find the objects in each Hidden Pictures puzzle.
Then check the Packing List on pages 30–31 to make sure you found everything.
"These apples look so good," says Kaboodle. "It will be hard not to pick too many!"
"The farmer gave us this basket to fill," says Kit. "We may need something else to hold the extra apples."
"I have something to help us hold the extra apples," says Kaboodle.
He looks in his backpack.
Happy reading!

BREAD
The Classic
KITTENS'
TASTY
TREATS

Kit and Kaboodle want
to bake a dessert.

"What should we bake?"
asks Kaboodle.

"My favorite dessert is pie," says Kit.

"Let's make an apple pie!"
says Kaboodle.

"That is a great idea!" says Kit.

"We have flour, butter, salt, sugar, and spices," says Kaboodle.

"There is just one thing we are missing."

"Apples!" says Kit.

"Do you know where
we can get the best apples ever?"
asks Kaboodle.

"Where?" asks Kit.

"At the farm down the road!"
says Kaboodle.

"Today is a great day to go to the farm," says Kit. "Let's get ready!"

Kit packs a few things.

Kaboodle packs a few things.
Then he packs more things.

"I hope I don't forget anything," says Kaboodle.

Sunscreen

Pencil

Baseball Cap

Water Bottle

Jacket

Thermos

Camera

Book

STUFF
JUNK
TOYS

Kit and Kaboodle arrive at the farm.

"We need to get apples," says Kit.
"But look at all the fun things we can do!"

"I've always wanted to go
through a corn maze," says Kaboodle.

"The maze is on our way
to the apples," says Kit. "Let's try it!"

"There are a lot of turns in here,"
says Kit. "I hope we don't lose our way!"

"I've packed a few things
to keep us on track," says Kaboodle.

He looks in his backpack.

"We made it out!" says Kit.

"That was fun," says Kaboodle.
"I'm glad we did the maze."

"Do you smell that?" asks Kit.

"It smells like doughnuts!" says Kaboodle.

"We can take a quick snack break," says Kaboodle.

"Fresh doughnuts are the best," says Kit. "But they can be messy."

"Don't worry!" says Kaboodle. "I brought some things we can use to stay clean."

He looks in his backpack.

Plate

Sink

Bar of Soap

Knife

Bib

Tablecloth

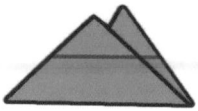
Napkin

Fork

DOUGHNUTS
TOTAL $2.42

"Yum!" says Kit.

"Those doughnuts were delicious."

"On to the apples," says Kaboodle.

"Look, it's a hayride!" says Kit.

"Maybe we can go for one ride," says Kaboodle.

"The farm looks beautiful from here," says Kaboodle.

"It does," says Kit. "But I'm starting to get cold."

"Not a problem!" says Kaboodle. "I packed some things to help us keep warm."

He looks in his backpack.

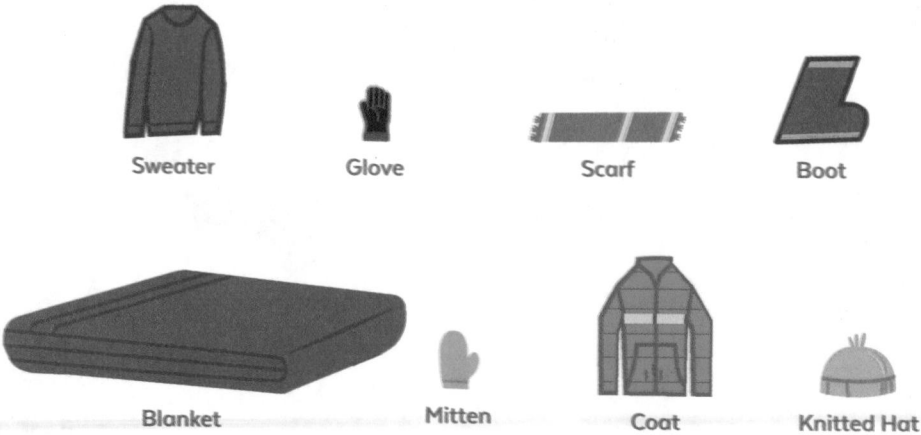

HAYRIDE

"Look!" says Kit.
"The hayride dropped us
at the apple orchard."

"There are so many kinds of apples,"
says Kaboodle.

"Those green apples are great for apple pie," says Kit.

"Let's pick them," says Kaboodle.

"These apples look so good," says Kaboodle. "It will be hard not to pick too many!"

"The farmer gave us this basket to fill," says Kit. "We may need something else to hold the extra apples."

"I have something to help us hold the extra apples," says Kaboodle.

He looks in his backpack.

Fanny Pack

Duffel Bag

Laundry Basket

Shopping Cart

Purse

Suitcase

Shopping Bag

Tote Bag

"These apples are going to make a great pie," says Kaboodle.

"Let's go home and start baking!" says Kit.

At home, Kit and Kaboodle make their pie.

Kit rolls out the pie crust.

Kaboodle cuts the apples for the filling.

They put the pie in the oven.

"The pie is ready," says Kit.

"It is delicious!" says Kaboodle. "We picked perfect apples."

"Going to the farm was a great idea," says Kit. "We did so many fun things."

"Where should we go on our next trip?" asks Kaboodle.

Trolley

Bus

Tractor

Ski

Airplane

Dump Truck

Scooter

Sailboat

SEPT
22
HELLO
MEOW
5:13PM

Did you find all the things Kit and

Airplane

Bar of Soap

Baseball Cap

Bib

Camera

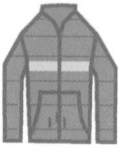
Coat

Compass

Duffel Bag

Glove

Jacket

Knife

Knitted Hat

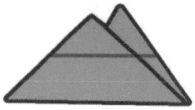
Napkin

Pencil

Phone

Plate

Shopping Bag

Shopping Cart

Sink

Ski

Tablecloth

Telescope

Thermos

Tote Bag

Kaboodle packed for their trip?

Blanket

Book

Boot

Bus

Dump Truck

Fanny Pack

Fork

Globe

Laundry Basket

Magnifying Glass

Map

Mitten

Purse

Sailboat

Scarf

Scooter

Spool of Thread

Suitcase

Sunscreen

Sweater

Tractor

Trolley

Water Bottle

Whistle

Harris County Public Library, Houston, TX

Copyright © 2021 by Highlights for Children
All rights reserved. Copying or digitizing this book for storage, display, or distribution in any other medium is strictly prohibited.

For information about permission to reprint selections from this book, please contact permissions@highlights.com.

Published by Highlights Press
815 Church Street
Honesdale, Pennsylvania 18431
ISBN (paperback): 978-1-64472-474-3
ISBN (hardcover): 978-1-64472-475-0
ISBN (ebook): 978-1-64472-476-7

Library of Congress Control Number: 2021938014
Manufactured in Melrose Park, IL, USA
Mfg. 09/2021

First edition
Visit our website at Highlights.com.
10 9 8 7 6 5 4 3 2 1

This book has been officially leveled with both the F&P Text Level Gradient™ Leveling System and the Lexile® Text Measure.

LEXILE®, LEXILE FRAMEWORK®, LEXILE ANALYZER®, the LEXILE® logo and POWERV® are trademarks of MetaMetrics, Inc., and are registered in the United States and abroad. The trademarks and names of other companies and products mentioned herein are the property of their respective owners. Copyright © 2021 MetaMetrics, Inc.
All rights reserved.

For assistance in the preparation of this book, the editors would like to thank Vanessa Maldonado, MSEd, MS Literacy Ed. K–12, Reading/LA Consultant Cert., K–5 Literacy Instructional Coach; and Gina Shaw.